This Scrapbook Belongs To:

Lady Ginny

Lady Ginny's Tea Parties

In memory of my lovely poodle, Ginny, and for Bill, Tom,
Keltie, Gail, the Walking Women and all the wonderful people
who contributed their favorite teaware.

Library and Archives Canada Cataloguing in Publication

Jolliffe, Susan
Lady Ginny's tea parties / written and illustrated by Susan Rennick Jolliffe.

ISBN 978-1-55143-398-1

I. Title.

PS8619.O499L33 2007   jC813'.6   C2007-901851-3

First published in the United States, 2007
Library of Congress Control Number: 2007924933

Summary: With all creatures, wild and tame, as guests, Lady Ginny the poodle and
Codger the cat are tea-party hosts extraordinaire.

Orca Book Publishers gratefully acknowledges the support for its publishing
programs provided by the following agencies: the Government of Canada through
the Book Publishing Industry Development Program and the Canada Council
for the Arts, and the Province of British Columbia through the BC Arts Council
and the Book Publishing Tax Credit.

Cover artwork: Susan Rennick Jolliffe
Jacket design: Teresa Bubela

Orca Book Publishers
PO Box 5626, Stn. B
Victoria, BC Canada
V8R 6S4

Orca Book Publishers
PO Box 468
Custer, WA USA
98240-0468

www.orcabook.com
Printed and bound in China.

10 09 08 07 • 4 3 2 1

Lady Ginny's Tea Parties

by
Susan Rennick Jolliffe

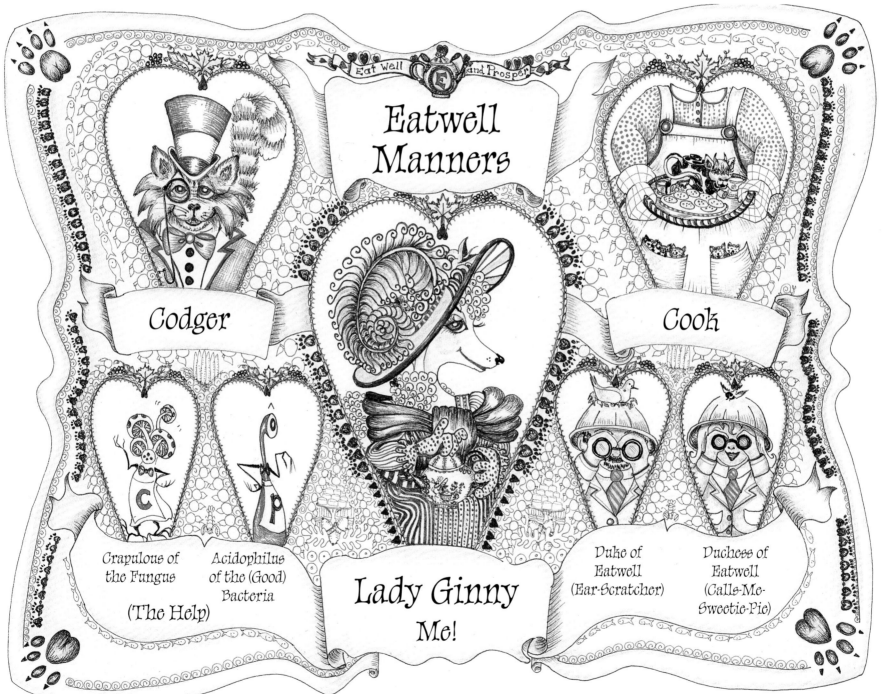

Eat well E and Prosper

Eatwell Manners

Codger

Cook

Crapulous of the Fungus

(The Help)

Acidophilus of the (Good) Bacteria

Lady Ginny

Me!

Duke of Eatwell (Ear-Scratcher)

Duchess of Eatwell (Calls-Me-Sweetie-Pie)

ORCA BOOK PUBLISHERS

Here I am looking gorgeous as usual but feeling kind of blue.

Ear-Scratcher and Calls-Me-Sweetie-Pie are still not back from their latest adventure. They were determined to explore the Tiny Township to see if the stories of wee flying horses were true.

We aren't really worried, because they love getting lost, but we miss them something awful. It's time for Eatwell's famous Tea Party Season to start and we are quietly building up to a We-Don't-Know-What-to-Do Dither.

Should Cook and I wait for them to return
and organize it like they always do? Or should
we go ahead and have the parties ourselves?
How hard can it be?

After all, I already have several new outfits.

Things to Do Today

Me: - Make a pile of Calls-Me-Sweetie-Pie's shoes out in the snow.
- Actually start to chew.
- Start a scrapbook.

Codger: - Tangle all of Ear-Scratcher's knitting wool.
- Invite over his annoying friends <u>again</u>.

Cook: - Make oodles of unnecessary food.

Guests for Tea Parties

Cats and Dogs
Bull Moose and His Ladies
Little Birds Returning
Frogs
Hummingbirds, Butterflies
    and Hummingbird Moths
Summer Night Feasters
The Herbivore Club
Canada Geese and Ducks
Winter Birds and Nutters
Forest Keeper Carnivores
Family

This is us getting ready for our first tea party. We are going to have the best parties ever, especially with me as the hostess with the mostest! So much to do, so little time. What shall I wear first? Cook filled the air with delicious smells, and Codger proved that he can actually be kind of cute sometimes.

This is me being excited.

This is Codger looking
unhelpful.

This is me telling Codger that
there will be little birds.

This is Codger looking
interested.

This is me planning
my wardrobe.

This is Codger looking unhelpful again.
He is suspecting there
will be work for him.

Things to Do Today

Me: - Be too excited.
- Try on ALL of my clothes.
- Write invitations.

Codger: - Mail invitations.

Cook: - Make amazing food.
- Set the table beautifully.
- Clean the house just
a bit.

JANUARY

The Someone-Forgot-to-Send-the-Invitations Tea

Guests: NO ONE

Teas: Bouillon Tea
         Catnip Tea

Menu: cheese spirals
        marrowbone cookies
        fish chorus cakes
        liver layer cake with
            chicken-lip icing
        Swiss-cheese squares
        cocktail weenies
        mouse rolls
        being miffed at Codger

Teaware: Family Favorite China

This was SUPPOSED to be the day of our first tea party . . . but we waited and waited and waited and NO ONE CAME.

I looked fantastic. Cook had set a beautiful table covered with yummy food. Codger looked suspiciously sheepish.

FEBRUARY

The Kitty-Spitty-Hot-Diggity-Doggity Tea

Guests: Cats and Dogs

Teas: Bouillon Tea
         Catnip Tea

Menu: cheese spirals
        marrowbone cookies
        fish chorus cakes
        liver layer cake with
          chicken-lip icing
        Swiss-cheese squares
        cocktail weenies
        mouse rolls

Teaware: Family Favorite China

"Got any doggie bags?"

"The cur bit me!"
"Did not, you hair ball!"

"Can I live here?"

"What happened to the mouse rolls? Nobody got any."

The relatives were our very first guests, and they licked every plate clean.

I thought it was a FABULOUS party! Don't you just love my hat?

Cook was not fond of the puppies on the table or the flying kittens.

Codger had way too much catnip, as usual.

MARCH

The Moostly Chomping Tea

Guests: Bull Moose and His Ladies

Teas: Labrador Tea
        Pond-Water Tea

Menu: horsetails
        watercress and pickled
            yellow pond-lily salad
        salt lick
        willow-twiglet bundles

Teaware: Blue Willow China

"Got any more lily buds?"

Rather quiet, the moose, except for the slurping and chewing. Not big on conversation. I'm embarrassed to admit that I was yawning when the antler came crashing down. Cook thought that it was time to move the parties outside and use sturdier dishes. Codger kept on pretending to be asleep.

APRIL

Welcome Home Twittery Tea

Guests: Little Birds Returning—
Robins, Bluebirds, Red-winged
Blackbirds, Song Sparrows, Flickers,
Ruby-crowned Kinglets
and Black-and-white Warblers

Teas: Springwater Tea
          Sap Tea

Menu: seed cake
          peanut-butter cookies
          housefly pie
          jellied grubs
          ants on a log
          dew worms
          nyger seed-suet Ding Dongs

Teaware: Cake Stands and Birdbaths

Here we are outside in the Sumac Gazebo, full of food, flirting, flitting and singing folk songs! Who minds a little rain when you are right in the middle of a romantic musical? Aren't my oilskins cute? Cook thought it was great fun. Codger just smiled a lot and drooled on his oven mitts.

MAY

The Jeepers Peepers Pond Party

Guests: Frogs: Spring Peepers,
               Leopard Frogs and Bullfrogs

Teas: Pond-Scum Algae Tea

Menu: balloon'o bugs
           shoofly balls
           mayfly mist
           red wigglers
           lazy larvae

Teaware: Plastic Dishes that Float

"Were we supposed to eat the bats?"

"Leaping lily pads, it was fun!"

Our Frog Tea Party went swimmingly! I looked spectacular in the old Dragon Boat.

The escaping food looked happy. Cook looked smashing in her hip waders.

Codger looked annoyed.

JUNE

The Tranquility Tea

Guests: Hummingbirds
   Butterflies
   Hummingbird Moths

Teas: Nectars of
    Catnip
    Dandelion
    Dame's Rocket
    Daisy
    Canada Anemone
    Mallow
    Pasture Rose
    Columbine
    Vetch
    Hedge Bindweed
    Butterfly Weed
    Scarlet Lychnis

Menu: rotting fruit compote

Teaware: Wedgewood Fountain

What a lovely day! The butterflies were heavenly, making polite conversation with their dancing. I don't speak butterfly, unfortunately, so I didn't understand what they were trying to tell me, but no matter. The hummingbirds didn't even dive-bomb each other too much. Don't I look absolutely beautiful? Cook was very relaxed. This time the catnip tea calmed Codger. He wrote poetry rather than batting at the guests.

"Had a reeking good time!"

"Loved those escargoings."

JULY

The Twilighty Flightly Tea

Guests: Summer Night Feasters—
Skunks, Raccoons, Bats and Bear

Teas: Iced Compost Tea

Menu: grub honeyballs
         napping luna moths
         crayfish roulettes
         moth flyby
         clammed ups
         escargoings

Teaware: Polypore Fungi Plates
         Pitcher Plants
         Firefly Samovar

"We Protest—The Luna Moth League."

"As good as garbage."

"Great food, but kind of stinky."

A magical warm summer night full of howling and swatting and swallowing. The crickets entertained us, and the fireflies gave us light. I was so comfortable that I imagined I could smell Calls-Me-Sweetie-Pie near, even over that Other Smell. We discovered that Codger has a really weird howl, sort of like he is in pain. Quite horrible, actually.

AUGUST

The Neighh-borhood Herbivore Tea

Guests: The Herbivore Club—
Palominos, Deer, Rabbits and
Groundhogs

Teas: Chamomile Tea
Springwater Tea

Menu: apples-in-a-bucket
carrot castles
parsley pinwheels
clover clusters with
dandelion dainties

Teaware: Bunnykit Dishes

This party was the only one that Cook was nervous about. Our farm folk are charming and gentle but really really picky about their food.

Cook picked, then arranged the food only seconds before our guests arrived so that everything was wonderfully fresh. A crunchiferous success!

I looked adorable. Cook was proud. Codger is particularly partial to palominos.

SEPTEMBER

The Honking Good Time Tea

Guests: Canada Geese and Ducks

Teas: Fastwater Tea

Menu: crispy rice squares
        slugs-in-a-blanket
        petites puffballs
        niblet cakes
        new grass tablecloth

Teaware: Airline Trays and Sinks

"Quacked me up!"

Lots of touch-and-go, to-ing and fro-ing flying practice. The geese and ducks were all in excellent humor and being very silly as they tried to teach us to fly! I flapped my paws, elegantly of course. Cook thought it was hilarious. Codger believed that he could actually feel himself taking off.

Bon Voyage to our brave friends.

OCTOBER

The Berry Nutty Joyous Tea

Guests: Winter Birds and Nutters—
Cardinals, Waxwings, Chickadees,
Blue Jays, Mourning Doves, Mice,
Chipmunks and Squirrels

Teas: Pumpkin Tea

Menu: serviceberry sandwiches
nyger seed-suet Ding Dongs
chanterelle mushroom tartlets
walnuts
acorns
wild grapes
sunflower seeds
highbush cranberry cookies

Teaware: Pumpkin Gourds, Turkeytail Plates

"Do you deliver?"

WE FOUND EAR-SCRATCHER
AND CALLS-ME-SWEETIE-PIE!!!!

Apparently they have been home for ages, still enjoying their holiday being tiny, and everyone knew but US! Squirrel thought it was too funny. Cook and I don't agree. I'm afraid that Codger's purring and my somewhat noisy cavorting in the leaves drowned out the rest of the party, and when I finally looked up from kissing Calls-Me-Sweetie-Pie, ALL of the food and ALL of our guests were GONE. I was kind of embarrassed for neglecting my hostess duties, but we were just SO EXCITED!

"Can I help you with your squirrel problem?"

NOVEMBER

The Something-to-Sink-Your-Teeth-Into Tea

Guests: Forest Keeper Carnivores—
Lynx, Wolf, Owl, Mountain Lion,
Fox, Mink, Otter and Wolverine

Teas: Pink Tea

Menu: snowshoe hare paté
         mouse wieners
         oeufs domestique
         stolen chicken sandwiches
         partridge puffs
         crow pie
         squirrel squares

Teaware: Fallen Antler and Snowshoe
         Platters, Horn Cups, Cow Tea Set

"Loved the paté!"

"More live food next time."

I was so happy to have Ear-Scratcher and Calls-Me-Sweetie-Pie back that I must admit I didn't see the crow and squirrel attack coming. They were offended by the Forest Keepers' hunting stories and the menu. I did sympathize. Cook did as well, and she was also a little concerned about the way some of our guests were looking at our lovely little bite-sized people.

Codger thought it was the best party he had ever been to.

DECEMBER

The Happiest Holiday Tea

Guests: Lady Ginny (me), Codger, Cook,
     The Duke and Duchess of
       Eatwell Manners (Ear-Scratcher
       and Calls-Me-Sweetie-Pie)

Teas: Earl Gray Tea
        Catnip Tea
        Bouillon Tea

Menu: snowflake pound cake
        bundt cake
        crumpets
        watercress and cream-cheese
          sandwiches
        sundried jerky rolls
        petits fours
        fishballs
        candied orange peel
        lots of hugs

Teaware: Family Fancy China

Joy to the World and Us!

MAKE YOU BIG AGAIN POWDER

What a year we've had! We had entertained most of the families of the Eatwell Estate, and now it was time for us. Cook and Codger and I were just bursting to give Ear-Scratcher and Calls-Me-Sweetie-Pie their Big Present. We gave them Make You Big Again Powder!

And it worked!

Dear Lady Ginny, Cook and Codger of Eatwell Manners,

We are pleased to announce that you have won this year's Tea Cup!
Your parties were the most unusual and creative of all the many entries.
They also looked like the most fun!

Choosing just the right food for each of your extraordinary guests
must have been quite a challenge. Congratulations to you, and our
compliments to the Duke and Duchess for gracefully remaining
in the background and for sending in your splendid scrapbook.

Well done!

The Tea Grannies

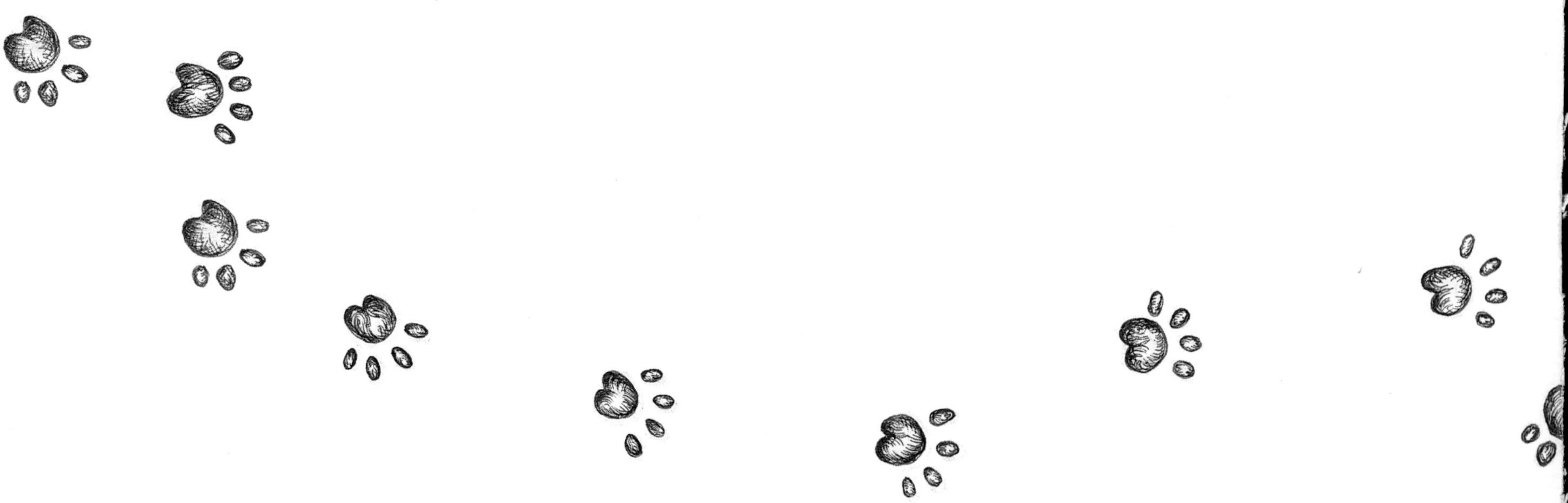